THE FALLING SKY

by

Jack A. Baret

DORRANCE PUBLISHING CO., INC.
PITTSBURGH, PENNSYLVANIA 15222

ISBN # 0-8059-4473-7
Printed in the United States of America

First Printing

For information or to order additional books, please write:
Dorrance Publishing Co., Inc.
643 Smithfield Street
Pittsburgh, Pennsylvania 15222
U.S.A.

Dedication

To my beautiful wife, Maryuri, who inspired me to publish; and whose patience and kindness helped me complete this book. And to my father, Angelo, Prince of the Zodiac.

MAX ORDERED ANOTHER espresso and returned to the task of writing to his friend who lived in Cuba. The café was spotted with a few patrons loyal to this establishment in the heart of the city.

All roads lead to Rome, he thought, or Paris or Amsterdam or New York or Toronto!

For years he had wondered what it would be like to live as a carefree citizen of the world in a cosmopolitan city like Paris. Now that he was here in the City of Lights, he had fallen in love with that solitary hour at dusk, between six and seven. When the last few rays of light trickled through the sheltering clouds and down onto these dots called human beings was the time when Max found happiness.

He was most creative during the evening hours, and so he found time to paint scenes of the street from his small balcony overlooking a cobblestone street. He managed to capture the hazy hues of weather-beaten houses which lined the boulevards, the rain-soaked streets, and the wrinkled faces of the older French—a mixture of character and pathos. All this was done in watercolor if he felt ambivalent or in oil if he was determined to capture a mood.

How ridiculous. Nothing is fixed for long. Everything changes to become the same again, he contemplated.

For a moment he grew sad as he remembered how his love had blossomed for a while and then withered. His girlfriends had always been passionate in their confessions of undying devotion to him. Nevertheless, this he knew to be transitory. He knew true love didn't last forever. It was a necessary affliction of the human condition. Man had to attend to other important matters besides being enraptured in pure love. At this moment what was of paramount importance to Max was ordering another espresso from his good friend Paul, the waiter.

"Paul, have you noticed how gloomy it's been around here in the last few weeks?"

"Yes, I have, but it's pointless to go on about the weather unless it's a hurricane warning! What difference can it possibly make? Gray skies, sunny skies, cloudy skies mean nothing to me. I am here in Paris, the hub of a wheel which spins and goes on with or without me. That will be three francs. No, make that four because I know you will order one more, and I won't charge you if you order a fifth espresso, which, in all probability, you will," added Paul.

"You're feeling rather philosophical today, and lucid, I might add, my friend. Perhaps you can explain why this is my happiest time of the day and yet the saddest time as well," he said as the glass-enclosed lanterns suddenly illuminated the dark corners of the street where the café was situated. "Perhaps you have struck real gold this evening, the golden paradox of life. We all crave to be free of our petty human foibles, and yet where would we be without them?" he said in a semi-arrogant tone.

"I'm sorry, Paul, but I don't follow your...."

"The only way we can compare our moments of joy is when they are up against the sadness. When you feel delight at the sunset or the warm afterglow left by a sunny day, you only realize its value after it abandons you. During the evening when the shadows are cast and forged on your mind forever you know how grounded you are. You, Maximillian Basset, belong here with your friends at this café in Paris. Nevertheless, these moments of tranquillity are ephemeral at best. Memories of times of your life transform you to some perfect afternoon. When you reach out to grab hold of it, it eludes you. You want to arrest and possess the moment you thought was the happiest moment of your life, yet it continuously haunts you until you feel the melancholy rise in your heart until it reaches your throat and chokes you to despair."

"What are you driving at? Am I to think all of this happens each day between six and seven when I feel the most peaceful?" Max intimated in a confused voice.

"No, but it's what you want to feel if you're alive. It's what we all feel but can't put into words. You are not alone, my friend, when it comes to the sadness of the human heart. I visit this domain every day when I look at my wife's photograph on the dresser. She died five years ago, and I have been in mourning ever since," confessed the waiter.

"My condolences. How have you managed without her?"

"In a way she liberated me from my responsibility to anyone other than myself. I am basically a selfish person and have to have things my own way. But I am changing, I hope."

"But didn't you depend on her love? I mean, you must have gotten used to her being around like a good friend to talk to about everything," Max admitted.

"You haven't been listening. I was and still am a selfish man. I was passionately in love with my wife because I thought I could wrest from her something I see in me. I forgot she was another person with her own soul and thoughts. I only realized this when she was gone. Then it was too late. As always, life teaches us these cruel lessons when the person or thing we love has vanished. This is the most costly insight we can attain. It comes at a very high price. To avoid this unnecessary hardship we must live as if we are not afraid of discarding the baggage we carry from the past," professed the middle-aged waiter.

"But this is very hard to do! We all come from somewhere, with a history of experiences and ideas," stated Max.

"Yes, but you must struggle and rub elbows with the nature of the beast. You should not be afraid to release your inner joy because it could be taken away at a moment's notice. The young at heart know this. They are too young to know what regret and suffering are. They can teach you the meaning of being here and alive, of being a slave-master. We are all slaves to certain passions, but we can master them by letting them become consumed by their own fires. Why have I never seen you with a woman? Come with me tonight, and I will take you to a brothel where the women are exceptional. You should get rid of all this baggage you're carrying around, or you'll become old before your time," concluded the waiter.

"Some other time perhaps. Tonight I will go for a walk through the streets, before sunset. I need inspiration for a painting I'm working on. Goodnight, my friend. See you tomorrow night, same time." Max slowly made his way around the corner of a street until he disappeared.

The evening had a slight chill, so Max bundled up in his green coat, pulling up the collar in defiance of the winter wind. The owners of the many cafés and stores which spotted the winding streets of this grand old city had already pulled down their steel doors and locked up for the night. The only places open were the bars and hotels. Max finally headed into a local bar for a cognac. He sat down and enjoyed his spirited drink. As is customary in these places, he was approached by a prostitute. Recalling the advice of his friend Paul, he made a place for her at his table. He introduced himself and the small talk began.

"Do you come here often?" he said quietly.

"Why are you whispering? There are no secrets here. I am a prostitute. Shall we go to my place?" she demanded.

"Slow down please! Can we just talk for a while?" Max retorted.

"I'll have to charge you for it after the first half hour," she said in an amateurish manner.

"That will be fine. Where are you from, and why do you live in Paris?" he began.

"Well, I'm from the Bordeaux region, and just like the wine from there, I go good with food. Will you please order me a sandwich; I'm starving," she implored the inquisitive Max.

"Why sure! Waiter, please bring this lady a cheese sandwich. I will have another cognac. Did you know you have a cocky smirk when you are listening to me? I find that very seductive."

"You're a queer sort. Why don't you want to make love to me? Men and women line up around the corner to have me. Yet you just want to talk," she bragged.

"Perhaps later, but for now I want to get to know you as a person," Max insisted.

"Well, I have no political or religious views, and I'm easily confused in intellectual conversations. I think about how much money I will make in a week so I can pay my rent and then spend the rest on food and clothes. I love to walk on the beach with the sand under my feet and the sea mist spraying against me and catching me by surprise. Oh! I love to read gossip magazines even if they aren't true," she quickly added.

"That's it? I mean, that is the extent of your life?" said the bewildered Max.

"I suppose you're some important rocket scientist or something?" she defended herself.

"No, just a person like you. You must want something more out of life than the eternal drudgery of your routines. Don't you want to escape from all of this?"

There was a long pensive moment when both of them stopped talking. They were collecting themselves from each other and withdrawing from the relationship, which was obviously mismatched. Like two strangers, each asking the other one for directions, they were both lost on these crossroads at the hub of the world. All the roads led out of Paris, but they both knew that the same roads which left the confines of their world eventually brought them back to it. They were stuck with each other, each wanting to leave and at the same time wanted to stay and enjoy the few moments they had with each other. The wheel of the world was turning, but they were at the hub and standing still. Maybe the world would go on without them, but for the moment they represented the focal point of being. They paid the price of meaninglessness by at least trying to be human beings, whatever their perspectives on life. He was a struggling painter and she an accomplished prostitute. It didn't make a difference what they did but how they did it. Morality is left behind in these cases, and God is distant though still watching. We are left on our own to live as we know best. Nobody seemed to be getting hurt from this situation. What was odd was that Max and Marie talked to each other with respect, like two good friends. Maybe they could be lovers?

It was getting late. Max paid Marie for her time, as promised, and walked, slightly inebriated from the four or five cognacs at the bar. However, he was sober enough to find his way home to his tiny apartment by following the unique landmarks en route—a store sign here, a weather vane there, one more lamppost which was painted an odd color, and finally the long climb up the stairs by the river to the street on which his flat was situated.

This particular evening had a strange aura about it. The sky had finally cleared, and despite the many bright city lights which obscured his vision, Max could make out the canopy of stars which guided him home. They were like a river of bright spots staring down on him and judging his every move. They were like God's vigilant vanguards ahead of some secret movement which waited for his command. It was a battle against time and space. Those had become Max's enemies. He felt that the boundless depth of space and endless days facing him were somehow going to defeat him if he dwelt on his human limitations long enough.

Like the curve of the bay and the smiles of the sea near the town where he was born, everything—the world, the planets, the stars, the approving smile of Marie—played an important role in affirming his existence here in the City of Lights; the harmonious convergence of these events which, if he hadn't thought about them, would not have even occurred to him. There was purpose behind them. In their perfect alignment; the heavens, stars, planets, sun, and earth, God had ordered them to be that way so Max could wrest some meaning from them.

The circles he traveled in, the people along the path he walked each day were the planets which revolved around him. Perhaps Marie was one of the stars which shone on the horizon. There were certainly enough of them out there. One of them had to have been born for him. His next quest would be a romantic one: to find his star in Paris.

He fell asleep as soon as he lay his head on the pillow. He dreamt that night of the home he had grown up in as a child and teenager. It was a crystal clear day and his mother had just hung the wash out to dry. The large white sheets flapped in the wind on the hill overlooking the bay. The whiteness and purity of those clean sheets washed away any doubts about why he was in Paris. The sun peeked between the clothes on the line and seduced his innocent curiosity toward worlds not yet discovered, not yet imagined. He knew he was destined to capture perfect moods like these. He painted them and enshrined them on canvas.

When he awoke he was eager to return to his work, to his painting. Many times he walked along a street which came to a fork. There he would stare for hours, undecided. Should he turn left or right? This ambivalence carried over from his youth as he could never decide on an ice cream flavor or the color of a girl's hair. At the time it had seemed like an insurmountable dilemma; now that he was mature he worked with it.

He felt fortunate to have survived many ordeals which had brought him close to death. A car accident which killed one friend and put another in a coma left him with a sore back and few cuts and bruises. This prevented him from a professional life in sports, so he decided to pursue the arts. Being rejected by a lover created an emotional scar which ran deep but was not permanent.

Out of suffering the heart grows deeper and more aware of life. One becomes insane or draws closer to God.

After doing some preliminary sketches of a street perspective he had been thinking about, Max turned to more mundane matters. He had let himself go for some time now, so he decided to take better care of himself. He made strong coffee and left for the barber.

He looked forward to meeting the patrons there, as they reminded him of characters from an old black and white movie. They seemed to converge there whether they needed a haircut or not. They would talk about everything and nothing in particular. The conversations ran the gamut: philosophy, politics, religion, or when to extract a soufflé from the oven. These were topics, of course, which would incite violent passions to collide in differences of opinion until the peaceful barber was forced to eject the truculent debaters from the premises. Max walked in and caught the tail end of a discussion.

"What do you mean? You must marinate the horsemeat overnight in rosemary, garlic, and olive oil! Stupid, don't shake your head like that. I know because I used to live on a farm as a child. I watched my mother cook all the time," said a burly man sporting a dark green suit.

They would discuss their petty differences over strong coffee and pastries and finally strike a truce after they were sufficiently satiated. Max never participated as a rule. However, today he felt especially confident.

"What should be of paramount importance is the removal of blood from the animal. Then pound it until tender. When ready to cook add a little seasoning and grill to your particular taste. *Violà*, and serve with a hearty merlot!"

His friends were stunned at this primadonna who told them how to cook. However, Max noticed his presence was no longer appreciated, so he made his escape into the street.

After a long pensive walk he stopped in front of a cathedral to gaze up at its impressive façade. Memories of being in church while growing up in Quebec, not all of them pleasant, flooded his mind until he felt dizzy with elation. He had always carried mixed emotions when it came to his beliefs about religion. This had nothing to do with his personal god. A religious god was an oxymoron as far as he was concerned. Religion had nothing to do with God. People, religious people, distorted the truth about God. Max had broken from the church since his youth had left him with bitter memories. He recalled abusive priests and nuns who would strike alter boys and sexually exploit students rather than instill proper virtues.

The journey to find his own personal god began when Max left the religious community of his youth to travel and find himself. However, the desert is large and arid, that is, the desert in man's soul. Though he traveled far and wide, he ended up here on the streets of Paris. He was no closer to happiness than he had been when he was at home. The heart grows deep, and in reflective interludes during the day, he resigned himself to stop asking a myriad of questions concerning his existence. Perhaps it was wiser to live without guilt. Why not? He was a good person. He discharged himself of all guilt and proclaimed innocence. He was free.

Yet now he was condemned to freedom. Freedom from the slavery and persecution man is able to wage against man is one thing, but freedom from a god who put man in this world to work and struggle and in the end pit man against a scornful Creator was quite a bit to swallow. Max decided not to contemplate matters beyond his intellect. That was for neurotic geniuses. He was more practical and down to earth. His pleasures were better appreciated when they were enjoyed without thinking about them too much. His passions would violently erupt and subside, when it came to the pleasures of the flesh. What good would it do to second guess nature's way? As sure as there was pleasure in the things he enjoyed doing suffering was not far behind. He couldn't have one without the other. The sooner people realized the duality of life, the less depressed they would get. Max chased the clouds away for the time being. Nevertheless, sooner or later, when he found himself alone and detached from humanity, the pain of living would return. It was living with a broken heart which was the unbearable part.

Knowing that many are unable to search for an authentic existence means one is left without a map, without an idea of finding oneself and that which makes one content. Max was not such an individual. His waters ran deep. It was the superficial people around him who provided him with the means to probe the human heart. He knew much of his journey meant suffering. This opened his heart to knowledge of the world and its circuitous routes.

Anyone with character is brought back to familiar paths and familiar experiences. With clenched teeth Max had braved many hardships. Instead of becoming cruel and ruthless, he had turned the world's hardness inward to the center of his being. He found the soul to be limitless in generosity and kindness if one wanted to accept this truth. It could also be a place of turmoil and misguided passions. One simply had to decide which way to live.

A garrulous person tortures others pointlessly with petty complaints and persecutions. Magnanimous people turn inwardly when the world is against them. Their patience is long and their memories short. They know how to live in the Now. This was how Max wanted to live, innocent of his predecessor's sins but not ignorant of their faults. The world needed work, and so did people. Max would set an example for everyone who cared.

He charged into the night, a leader of men, still on the go, painting scenes which captured the spirit on canvas. It was all an illusion but one worth chasing until one met his or her maker. God wove the magic imperceptibly, and Max's vocation was to arrest it in still life: here a mother with baby, there a rain-soaked street which reflected the blurred neon signs. It was lonely to be this detached from the world, but it gave him the perspective to make the final leap, the leap which would carry him beyond the edge of his known world, past the confines of the little bars and cafés, above the roof of the barber shop. His wish was to extol reality to the highest degree, in his life and art.

Max had been sleeping well lately. One night he had dreamt of many disconnected scenes: an old girlfriend paying him an endless supply of money, another one revealing her bosom in a seductive dance. Suddenly the nightmares had returned, signs and omens of death had stuck in his mind when he had awoken and he languished over the prospect of a disrupted reality, one which kept him from realizing his potential. There was some unfinished business in his psyche, but how could he get at it and purge it from his tormented soul forever?

Such wisdom could only be found with a woman. They were the real carriers of an intuition and knowledge not easily found in the world. They knew the way to the netherworld; they were the gatekeepers of the soul. A special woman was required to open the floodgates of anger and resentment from his troubled youth, unleashing and purging Max of this evil. This woman was the prostitute, Marie.

He seemed to be searching endlessly for someone who understood him and would not abandon his cause. The search always began and ended with ambivalent conclusions. Women were open-ended conduits of pleasure and beauty who took one on a journey of good intentions, which led directly to the gate of hell. This was the season of suffering. If one didn't suffer, one missed the point of life, an appreciation that the trappings of death and misery lurk around each corner.

Naturally, like most of us, Max had his escape mechanisms. Good food, wine, and women, while they lasted, were capable of helping Max avoid the pain of a withdrawal from reality. Sooner or later, memories would flood in to remind him of the limitations of the soul. The values people imposed on themselves prevented freedom from flourishing beyond certain limits. A moral person was not as free as he or she thought. The rewards were small; virtue being its own reward lasted briefly and was forgotten. Instead humans remembered the evil and atrocities rather than the good will. It must have been a morbid fascination with the inevitability of death that drove many to a life of hedonism. Max preferred to battle the flesh with the spirit.

He would live as if he already joined the spirit in the sky, the place to which we soar when we die. That meant not hurting anyone deliberately. However, in order to stay truly free, Max intended to live beyond the morality imposed on him by mere mortals. Living a detached existence let him keep his horizons open. The borders of his soul were open to experimentation and expansion. A person with morals and values had closed borders. This did not mean one should not set limits for oneself. It simply meant once those limits are found, they could be suspended for a final judgment. In any case, people crossed them, back and forth, living on the edge, on the precipice of good and evil, yet transcending the fixed morality imposed by their ancestors.

There was a knock on the door. It was Marie, and her provocative dress drove Max to distraction. He had to leave his work, even though the paint was drying quickly, in order to make mad passionate love to this harlot.

He grabbed her by force and set her on a table, spreading her legs and removing her stockings and panties while making pelvic thrusts into her womanhood. It was violent but gentle and passionate. Once it was over they leaned against each other, exhausted and panting in short erratic breaths which wheezed in delight. A light mist of sweat formed on their skin as a cascading light permeated the smalls of the apartment. It was Max's favorite time of the day, between the hours of six and seven. The world order was restored; it was perfect with or without God.

They fell asleep until the next morning. Max woke up first and prepared breakfast while Marie slept till noon. The first snow came in large flakes. Imperceptible at first, the only way to notice them was to stare at them through the window. Gradually they covered everything within their reach: the cars, signs, and street. The snow fell for quite some time until a new silence brought relief to those who needed blessed peace. For the rest it was a nuisance which kept them indoors, away from the maddening throngs of humanity which roamed the streets.

The Parisians needed a place to go when they were not making a living. They needed their cafés, restaurants, bars, and dance halls. Whether one was young at heart or broken hearted the streets provided a refuge from loneliness and despair. The many alleyways and walkways which criss-crossed the boulevards formed a world in itself. It was the escape out of the abyss from which many floundered from time to time. It was the heart of a city which renewed itself daily.

Max and Marie were thankful they no longer had to play the masquerade. They found each other, and the world outside disappeared, at least temporarily. Life went on without them, and people wondered why they no longer played the game of life as players on the world stage. The love they nurtured was enough to fill the dark, full nights. It was a spiritual dance which fulfilled the requirements of two beings who came into this world incomplete. One complemented the other; each filled in the missing colors which were lacking in the other.

His paintings seemed to come alive. The figures were no longer frozen in surrealism. They invited one to join in their frolicking, to walk along with them on the streets and in the parks. They begged their onlookers to sit with them in the bars and cafés. They invited audience participation. Marie noticed how his work seemed to be achieving a new standard of excellence.

"I really enjoy watching you work, Maxie. The people in the paintings seem so alive, as if they are really walking and talking. They remind me of the people we know in the bars," Max said.

"Yes, it's true. That was the whole point to the exercise." He pointed out and explaining the various characters in the painting he called Scenes from the Edge. "This old man with the cane would come into the barber shop and sit for hours without saying a word. He would just listen to the conversations. If you invited him to join in, he would look away as if he was holding some deep secret."

If the eyes are the window to the soul, then the soul is the gateway to a place beyond the world. Many of us harbour such places: deep dark secret places in our souls, which we rarely allow others to see. In this sanctuary are all the possibilities we could ever be, wrapped up in hopeful dreams and flying machines which carry us high above our mundane struggle to move mountains.

When Max looked at the old hunched-over man in the barber shop, Max saw a bit of himself struggling against age and reason.

The mystery of a person, the sanctity of each human being, lies in his or her ability to reveal and not conceal secrets. Secret invitations, those soft voices we wait forever to hear, guide us toward the source of existence.

The situation—the people in it are secondary and incidental—the core of being protects us from damage by an indifferent world which seeks an out, an escape from pain and suffering. Our universe, which stares back at us with pale blue eyes, wishes to displace us, in essence becoming who we are. We invent goals to surmount; we challenge the rock and mountains in order to postpone the inevitability of death, the great equalizer. We all fall the same way.

The next time Max saw the old man, Max knew the old man's silence was his last weapon against Father Time. Through his suspicious glances at the variety of people, the old man was simply holding on selfishly to the secrets of his soul. He was guarding those precious memories from being stolen by others who would probably distort his truth by gossip and bad storytelling.

Nonetheless, the eyes rarely lied. In the light they softened up and grew moist and pale like the sky before the rain begins. They had witnessed perfect mornings and delightful afternoons during which hope had sprung eternal and love had blossomed without pressure from time or purpose. Things happened because they happened that way.

There is not motive in being in love. The moment we think about why we love is the moment it loses meaning. This is when the night has won. We are forced to hide in the corners of the dark room; we retreat to that secret place of the soul, where nobody knows or sees us. This was the place to which the old man would go when he would leave the barber shop and take his metaphysical journey while his body stayed behind.

While Max worked on his painting, Marie was busy working on dinner in the kitchen. The people he was painting were absent, but their rare profiles left an indelible stamp on his mind. They seemed to be speaking to him from the quiet corners of his small flat. They needed someone like Max to free them from their loneliness, from their longing for escape beyond the city limits. Max was such a person; he would freeze them on canvas for eternity.

Once the sketches of the shadowy figures were complete and the colors added, his friends left the confines of the smoky barber shop and made the leap to his painting. Max saved them from the fall. He gave them immortality.

One night he invited them over for dinner and unveiled the painting for his first exhibition. They studied it for a while, and then smatterings of opinions broke out.

"Maxie, you make me look so old!" said the old man.

Nobody could believe he could speak as they turned to him in amazement. Somehow Max had given him a voice, rather a disembodied voice. Perhaps it was the character in the painting who was speaking and not the real person. In any case, they were all happy he finally had said something, and they resumed eating the lovely supper Marie had prepared.

The rest of the evening was spent discussing various topics like philosophy, art, and the real world. Frenchmen loved to lazily talk about anything, especially after a full rich meal. The burly bald man who was always impeccably dressed asked Max why he painted.

"Well, you see, it is to distract me from the ugly side of life: the pain, suffering, deceit, and misery. The students of psychology will tell you I had a bad childhood, so I mask my emotions by painting over them and sublimating their real intentions on canvas. However, my own reason has to do with capturing the fine line between beauty and the beast. If you look closely at the figures here, you will notice how slightly exaggerated their outlines are. I am trying to draw that fine edge between ugliness and beauty. I would say there is beauty in things or beings which seem ugly, even mediocre. One has to stretch the line of vision past the lines and angles which constitute a thing, place, or person," he concluded in a pedantic tone.

That evening, after everyone had left, Max dreamt a strange dream. Someone sawed in half a car he did not even own. However, toward morning a more symbolic dream occurred. In the second dream the characters of his latest painting, Scenes from the Edge, seemed to take on lives of their own. They became spiritual templates which drifted off the canvas and floated high above the middle of the room. They danced a macabre ballet of primitive proportions and surreal exaggerated form. They were beautiful monsters from down below. They were angels sent to rescue Max from his heartbreak. Their colors grew more friendly as they spun in ritualistic fashion, like the chorus girls of the burlesque shows. His mind was spinning round and round in an orgiastic attempt to join them. He reached out to grasp one of their appendages, but they disappeared as he awoke to realize it was just a dream.

Marie had awakened by now and turned to Max to find out what had disturbed him in his sleep.

He said he had been dreaming about the characters in the painting. "They must be monsters from my past, which have come back to haunt me! I wish sometimes I could just bury some of those bad experiences and the ugly feelings which go with them," he intimated to Marie.

"Perhaps they are rising again to the surface for a reason," she added.

"For what possible reason have they returned but to terrorize and frighten me? They're ghosts from my past."

"Maybe they are not ghosts. Maybe they are symbolic of an unresolved conflict with your father or priest or another strong paternal figure who disillusioned you."

He looked at her with caring eyes and knew how blessed he was to have such an insightful lover. He rolled over and climbed on top of Marie, while slowly removing her underwear. He gently mounted her with his permanent horn and pressed his turgid flesh on her ivory smooth skin. Max was so excited and warmed by her beauty that he climaxed quickly with a satisfying howl. He repeated the sexual acrobatics two more times until they both fell back in exhaustion. The bitter taste left in his mouth from the feelings aroused by his dream faded toward the overcast sky which loomed over his flat.

He sat up in bed, thinking about the characters form the barber shop. They grew in size until they became the constellations which formed his personality. Suspended there, high above the roof of his flat, were the gods and devils of his soul. He knew they were there to stay. Eventually he realized how necessary it was to deal with them as they appeared in life or in dreams. What was the difference? They seemed real while awake or asleep. He would have to confront each situation as it arose. These gargoyles which kept watch over his soul would dig their nails into the back of his neck and up into his brain until Max would collapse from fatigue. He had battled them all his life as if he had waged a private war with the friend or enemy within, the struggle between good and evil. His soul was the battlefield on which the spirit fought against the desires of the flesh. It was a crusade against the infidels of his soul, brought to the surface by the sins committed through his innocent brushes with evil.

Yet how did one bury a past which would not go away? In real time, past, present, and future coalesced under one mandate; learning how to survive. However, it was never enough just to survive. One had to get along with oneself and bargain with the devils of this world. In their desire to be immortal, they wished to conquer one's soul and leave the sins of the world behind. One had to be careful not to let them win over one's soul. Max was aware of these attempted coups and made sure neither time nor complacency, the two greatest enemies of the soul, would displace him from his mission.

The falling sky fell all around Max as he sat at his usual table, sketching on a small pad. Or was he the one who was falling? Falling from what and toward where? His private demons were descending from up above to his lair, the world below. It was a metaphysical inversion. God was here now in the world, and he wanted to push Max over the edge. Could Max pass the test? Was he ready to be transfigured into the superhuman realm, into being his own judge and executioner? To be finally rid of his death wish, to let God into his soul forever and cast out the demons which wanted to possess it, this was his only mission.

He knew what a woman could do for the soul, and Marie was definitely a woman. She could be a prostitute and virgin at the same time. She had an innocence which was uninhibited; she was unafraid to reveal herself and show her vulnerabilities. She cried like a child and hid herself for her man. She may have been anyone outside Max's flat, but when she was with Max his demons were paralyzed with fear. Something in a woman's soul held the secret of life. It contained the nectar of the gods.

Man only grew as tall as a woman's roots went deep. Max was anchored in the soil beneath the concrete jungle which was the streets of Paris. His feet would ache from roaming around the city for hours, looking for inspiration. Many times he would find a square and sit there wondering how lonely he was; what it was which had brought him here. Then he would go home, and a memory of his father or an old black-and-white photograph of him would trigger some tender feeling he had had for his father. The tears would roll down his face until he tasted the sweet saline solution secreted from his tear ducts.

His father had been a hard-working middle-class stiff who had needed to rest after he died. When his father was buried, Max had thought, What a well deserved rest. He had never even considered an afterlife or heaven or hell or Sheol for his father. The man needed to rest in a place without routine, a place where each day was born like the last—no schedules and no bills to pay.

The funeral already had been paid for in full. Now his father could stay in bed all day. There were no production quotas to meet or uptight foremen to scream at him for deadlines. What a life it was to be dead! Some day Max would join him, and they could share a glass of wine all day every day, leisurely discussing philosophy or fishing or whatever. For now, however, Max was alive and kicking.

Marie played a very special part in showing Max his finitude while guiding him infinitely beyond his own limits.

When the spirit and the flesh collide something very unique happens. Mountains fall to the sea, and earth is moved to make way for the peaceful transformation of love. In the purity of love are the properties necessary to make things happen. Max wanted to distill such properties from his relationship with Marie and bring them out in his work. He wanted to give his paintings the stroke of the sublime in characters which were quite ridiculous. In real life these people were ordinary, but their mediocrity was raised to the realm of the beautiful. With each lash of the brush, each poignant dab of color, every empty space filled the imagination with something it lacked: certainty.

We bend our eyes to see what isn't there. We stretch our imaginations to make reality better than what it is. What should stop us from living as if we were part of a surreal painting where the objects and figures combined under one eye, one mind, the idea of God? To praise reality until the scenes or situations within the frames of his paintings rebelled and usurped their unnatural borders and crossed into reality, this was what Max wanted to capture in his work. He wanted the people to see his paintings as an extension of what everyday reality, mediocrity, could be if people would only express themselves according to their authentic beings. By living behind a mask, the true identity of the soul languished in myth and taboo. By exaggerating the human form in art, Max could liberate the soul from suffering a useless fate.

Max could bend reality to suit his imagined perception of people and places, but when he was alone to face himself, the only truth staring back at him was the image in his mirror. He could alter the form and lines and change the rules which nature had intended, but he could not rely on reality to conform to his magic brush. It just didn't happen that way. Before he had met Marie he would spend countless hours sketching portraits of the ideal woman. First she would have the classical lines of a Venus di Milo, probably blonde, blue eyes, and her hair woven and neatly tucked behind a long ivory neck. Then he would feel more earthy and erotic, so he would draw an African woman with full lips, large hips, a succulent bosom, and velvety smooth skin. Gradually, after numerous alterations and erases with his dark pencil, he would end up with a rather average-looking woman, dark hair, penetrating eyes, and a full round figure. He then would give her a mysteriously timeless smile which expressed a longing to be understood and tamed. He must have been thinking of Marie.

In his dreams other women would appear and disappear in trails of vapor. He would follow them to the four corners of the world to know their secret powers, their longing to tame their wild spirits. He concluded that their love of men like him or anyone else was born down below. In the netherworld, love, desire, and lust were crystallized and raised to a higher purer form only after many trials and tests of endurance proved they were ready for immortality. This was the sort of love of which Max had always dreamed.

Perhaps Marie was such a woman, one who could challenge Max's profound need for a noble enduring love which transcended the fiery lusts of the carnal desires of the moment. Too many times he had confused the explosive passions of the flesh with the spiritual rebirth of his soul, which only a special woman could give him. He wasn't sure, but at first he noticed her as an illusive enigma in his dreams. He would search for her in crowds, in bars and cafés, in fruit markets, in the subway. He would get carried away, going from one end of the city to the other, often falling asleep in one of the subway cars. Suddenly some woman dressed up professionally in the latest fashion would catch his eyes. He would move toward her for a closer inspection, but she would slowly vaporize in the diaspora of the city.

These magical interludes kept him hopeful amidst the dying embers of burned-out romances and deserted dreams. Like loose flying papers which catch a whirlwind and move up toward the expanse of a limpid blue sky, Max's heart would ride the edge of such breezes until he escaped the pull of gravity. It was gravity which kept him on earth to face the eternal darkness, the heart of the beast. What was this marauding phantasm which lurked in the corners of his mind, waiting to spoil his happiness? He had to hunt it down and kill it once and for all. Perhaps it was nothing, something he had contrived with an absence of malice. Perhaps it was the evil in the world which was working on him, entering every pore in his body, usurping his goodness, or wanting to become just like him.

Perhaps it would be better to go his own sweet way. Marie had been with him, and she was a good companion, but she soon had become just so much window dressing, subject to the changing fashions. Why was everything always moving so fast? One's heart was in it, and then suddenly mood changes and market forces altered one's frame of reference.

In a life of static routine one could be catapulted beyond one's wildest imagination into cyclonic feelings full of teeth and turmoil. Max would feel these emotions and ride them to the end of the line. The people close to him, friends who knew him, would go along on these roller coaster rides and soon realize Max was escaping from something he called home.

What could have happened to precipitate these moments of anguish which dwelt on the past? Now, here in Paris, the past, present, and future seemed to radiate outwardly from the hub of the city. What was certain was that he was alive; this sum total of choices brought him here. The city, its lights, and its snobbish people provided a window onto a world of infinite possibilities. The future at times seemed already written, but it was not necessarily so. Everyone was subject to disaster and poor choices. Nobody was exempt from such fate. However, the unlived portions, the roads less traveled converged on some future place, a hopeful land where stars, long suspended and out of use, fell to earth to realize someone's dream. This place was Paris or Toronto or Hong Kong. What difference did it make where someone lived? One simply lived somewhere, and that was enough!

It was the middle of winter in Paris, and the rains came, bringing with them their billowy dark clouds. They seemed to bowl over the weak-spirited and melancholic ones. The other city dwellers took on these days without sun and silver lining with a certain tragic optimism.

Max invited the rains with open arms. He and Marie would lie in bed and listen to the soft tapping on the window pane. Suddenly the raindrops would increase in frequency and cascade down on the roof with a crash. The intermittent thunder jump started their hearts, sending a fresh wave of electricity throughout their bodies. The feeling grew in ecstasy, invigorating them with boundless energy. They used it to make love all afternoon until it was time to get up and make some dinner.

After these acrobatic episodes of Olympian love-making, Max would take Marie's hand, and together they would go for a walk on the wet sidewalks. The air was damp and cold while the moisture and vapor poured out of their nostrils. They looked like two wild horses freely roaming the concrete jungle.

Often they would stop to graze in some bistro along the way to their favorite café.

People react differently when they see two people in love. They smile when they see a couple walk by arm in arm, heart to heart. When the lovers press their bodies up against each other, they release tiny quarks of electricity. These quarks are so small and light they float up to the heavens. When enough of them are produced, they coalesce into a star, one's personal star which watches over and protects one from harm. However, one must be romantic enough to believe in such things. When one sees a falling star, one knows a romance is coming to an end.

Such a sad thought, one could say, but a falling star really is a blessing in disguise. For when it falls, when it dies, the star is reborn on earth as a human being whose job it is to find the soul mate. Max had found his and was determined to make it work.

All his life had been spent in loneliness, in so much toil and hardship. The time was now to pick himself up by the bootstraps and get on with living. He had never forgiven himself for surviving a tragedy in high school, in which someone had died and another person had been critically injured. It was as if he should have been the one to suffer their fates.

How cruel we are to each other, he thought. But we're even harder on ourselves!

It was time to let himself off the hook. In fits of anger and emotional confusion he would often blame others for his misgivings or, equally damaging, blame himself. Here in this city of innocent passions which slowly burned past midnight and brought the dawn of the age of understanding and love, Max had found happiness.

Being a generous man he wanted to share this knowledge with his lover and the world. The only way he knew was through his art and communication with friends. Everything else would fall into place.

Placing himself as an avant-garde contributor to the art world and intelligentsia of his time meant he had to be responsible for his freedom. Although he felt depressed at the state of the world, its misery, disease, and corruption, he was sure certain things would never change: man's inhumanity to man, the struggle between good and evil, and making peace with one's creator. All these causes seemed worthwhile to pursue as human projects; however, they were illusions at best unless you were able to internalize the various truths found in the world.

On balance, Max found much to be grateful for: the simple beauty, the primary biological pleasures, and dealing with human fate. Yet the ugliness and deceit often made him feel suicidal, and once when he was young and passionate, he had attempted it. He had blamed the psychotic relationship with his father, but it went much deeper than that. It went to the very core of being, to the heart of the darkness already in the universe.

He believed in order to know life one had to stare at death and all its putrid smells and ugliness. Shocking as it seems, Max accepted the tragedies and cruelties as if he already understood why man deserved to suffer. The guilt and inexorable pain was enough to fill any man. It was what one did with the ineluctable suffering which was important to Max. Finding out how one could turn it into something special and beyond this world should be the mission of every man. So Max turned to art as the purgation of his soul which was doomed to sin for just being in the world. Yet it was what Marie could do for his soul which really made everything worth living for. Woman possessed this quality of releasing the best man could be. This was not asking too much.

Max felt it was important to learn from a broken heart, from the suffering torment of unrequited love. He knew he was close this time to bridging the gulf between himself and the one he loved. For too long his intentions always had erupted in a paradoxical power play while trying so hard to love someone and not having the love returned in the same fashion.

In the end he would feel as if he had to climb a castle wall to reach the lover. He always felt he was on the outside, looking toward someone else's happiness. It was time to look on the inside and see where his relationship with Marie was going. He was tired of climbing castle walls and looking through windows. This opened the door to the real self, the self he had hidden for too long.

Who was this Max Basset anyway? I mean he was a man like most men, connecting with other human beings, some beautiful, some not so pretty, some fat or thin, tall or short, wise or blissfully ignorant and happy to be that way. I suppose Max was searching for some recognition of a higher purpose which would affirm that all he was doing was the right thing. That was all anybody could hope for.

Running away was not the answer. If we could constantly look over our shoulders, we would realize running away is an illusion. The moment is lost.

End of Part One

THERE WERE INDEED oppressive forces at work within this world, but one had the freedom to choose, every step of the way, the manner in which to respond to and deal with these forces. Max knew running away from the evil which tried to rule his soul was not the way a man should handle it. It made certain overtures, via the people of his youthful world, to make him feel guilty about himself. So it had taken him a long time to start feeling good and getting in touch with his real self.

He had begun to take his time with mundane routines to better understand how time was broken down into its smallest measure. After all, the true measure of a man was how he extolled reality, how he lifted himself out of the doldrums and into the arena with the gods and angels.

We all rise to certain occasions in order to meet our fate. Some of us were meant to freeze reality—certain scenes on canvas and so on—long enough so it could never run away. Beautiful moments, magic times like just before dusk in the evenings, and certain sunny days you think could never end. Reflective interludes at the café when life stands still in an eternal display of arrested time, when the flow of time ceased, and one is in perfect harmony with oneself and the world, Max thought.

Naturally if such slices of life could be captured, distilled, and bottled, everyone would race to the store to buy them. Max wanted to paint the window to such a world and share it with humanity. He found it easy to cruise into and out of the diaspora, spilling out the contents of his experience. He was Aquarius the Water Bearer.

One thing plagued his mind to distraction. The ambivalent feelings he held for Marie created a distance between them. Although she had always proved herself loyal to Max, she was not convinced he was totally committed. Perhaps he harbored resentment about her licentious past and could never forgive her. Maybe Max had never resolved certain conflicts from his tormented childhood. In all the outrages humanity had perpetrated against him, Max still had turned out to be a rather decent person.

"We are determined by the choices we make. All moments of truth trickle down into the sink of reality, collect there, decompose, and remain stagnant until they rematerialize into a higher purpose. We all must be headed for some special awakening in which everything becomes more lucid. In this life or another life; rather no, it had to come in this one!" he demanded, not realizing Marie had been listening to him muttering to himself.

"Why are you so hard on yourself, Maxie? Can't you just live and forget all the mysteries and puzzles? You have me now. Isn't that enough? You have your work. I think you ask too much of life. You are asking for impossible guarantees, beyond what life can deliver. Perhaps I should leave you to work out your problems because obviously you don't need me around. I think you love to be in your own misery. Just let it go. Put this anger about your tough upbringing to bed once and for all! It's a matter of choice. After all, tomorrow is another day, the day you learn to accept life the way it is," she intimated philosophically.

More bewildered than ever, Max plunged into his work, hoping it would distract him from the horrors of his past. He needed respite from the badness in him. His world was a world of pleasure, with his woman ahead of everything else; one or two other special people and all the other women were like some flavors of ice cream, each to be licked and savored until they are covered in a blanket of silvery saline saliva. Their smells and perfumes were intoxicating, and often he would sit at the café, waiting for the breeze to carry their pungent odors his way. It would be a mixture of sweat, vaginal excretions, and perfume, which would turn the staunchest stoic into a sexual madman.

It was madness Max was most afraid of. If knowledge was lord, he was certainly one of the disciples. Yet, paradoxically, he also knew finding what one searches for isn't always a wise thing. Perhaps it was best just to live day to day as if one was not accountable for one's sins. After all, wasn't that what judgment day was for? If we are already born guilty for the sins of our predecessors who breached a contract with God, what would be the point of pretending we could ever wipe the slate clean? Perhaps we could for a brief period; then it would start all over again. The vague commitment to living pure and absolved of sin and vice, the promises we all run away from because we are afraid we are going to lose out, all are exercises in self-delusion because we know the good things are also immersed in the bad. Why should we feel guilty about feeling good when feeling good means crossing certain taboos?

The knowledge of good and evil transcends life itself. It is suspended there, between heaven and earth, in the mind and body of humanity. How we use it determines our character and virtue. If we abuse this privilege, we fail to be truly human. Being human for Max meant expanding the old horizons of experience beyond their present existence. Whether in his work or play, Max knew the only way to win his heart was to convince it with the strategies of the mind. The body would naturally follow this lead.

So where was Max's mind leading him? It seemed to move in strange circles, now thinking about how nice it was to be loyal to one woman, then pondering numerous sexual liaisons with three, four, or five women simultaneously or each one separately.

Just as in real life, his dreamworld involved various incongruous episodes which lacked a thread of continuity. He needed to be grounded in some belief that happiness was around the corner once he overcame the incessant melancholy of everyday living.

He used to dream of flying like an eagle over mountains and through valleys until he reached the sea. In these dreams Max felt free, with the weight of the world off his shoulders. However, he hadn't had one of those dreams for a while, and he missed the idea of being free from responsibilities. Just managing to survive by eking out a living from his paintings preoccupied him constantly. With Marie helping him now, he could afford to sit in the squares and cafés and do nothing.

Life was certainly absurd and death the steady reminder of the meaninglessness and futility of our endeavors. Max was feeling trapped by his labors as if they had dragged him to his duty of holding up a mirror to humanity.

"See, this is what you look like! Don't you see and know who you are, you mediocre bourgeois lot?" he realized.

Nobody was listening except Marie. She seemed to be the only one who really appreciated the way he felt. She was far from mediocre. In fact, she extolled reality for Max. Where would he be without the chalice to hold up that limpid blue sky? Marie was the holy chalice from which Max drank. It overflowed with her juice. It was an everlasting love. Pure love is immortal, to keep forever, whether in this world or not. The love we share is never right or wrong and good or bad; love draws us toward each other, so we are sheltered from the dark.

In the vast empty space of the universe, Max searched for, or perhaps always knew, a star was meant for him. He had to see it and know what it meant. Humanity could not provide the answer, for down here, through the ages, good men were lost in searching for something permanent. When they tired of one thing they moved on to the next, never satisfied and gradually losing hope. Max didn't have to look far. That search did not have to take him too far. The world beyond was merely an illusion. This world of fire, stone, and water, sun and song, spirit and flesh was one which he would never trade for anything. Despite his many ordeals, his tormented soul and melancholy, his youthful spirit kept him young at heart, eager to know that in being alive one is still on the move and ready to face the night.

Max was a pioneer of the human spirit, while engaged in the noble cause of bringing the vision of humanity down to earth for everyone to enjoy. He praised his fellow man and saw him, despite his many failings and foibles, as a miracle invention of flesh, bone, and spirit. Far above the maddening throngs of humanity was a reason for people to lift themselves out of the doldrums of iniquity, poverty, and suffering. It lay with a struggle to understand that with each fresh start is a chance to conquer death and put it in chains forever. Max loved life too much to allow death to keep him down. In a bold stroke or even with an empty white space on canvas, he captured the fleeting sense of time and space, frozen in a simple painting until the curious gaze of an onlooker gave it new life.

What did a person do with all the afternoon interludes in which moments slipped through the fingers no matter how hard one held onto them? Max harvested days like this. Some he stored in the closet, some went into the catacombs of memory, and some would return with a will of their own. Often the face of a girl or part of a scene would arrive at an inauspicious time. Part of a thought, broken off from some past memory, would leach into his brain to remind him how human he was, how the past never went away but was part of the present and future. Then he would experience deep pensive moods in which he wondered, What if things were different? What if I could have changed the outcome of a bad experience? How ridiculous, he thought. There is no way to do that. We must accept the immutability of time. Certain things can never be altered once done. Yet time itself marches on and yields to its weaker transitoriness.

Max glanced at his watch. It was time to hit the streets during his favorite hour of dusk: when the sun set and surrendered its myriad hues to a falling sky which welded the horizon to a tired old earth. Time was slipping through his hands and pores and every other opening of his body. Yet, as if by osmosis, he became revitalized during this magical time of the day. He was able to absorb the last bit of light escaping the atmosphere, while his shriveled up soul welcomed the boost.

As he sat on a park bench to observe the passing of day into night, he contemplated the very mystery of life, how unknown possibilities grew into the fruits which would sustain him for the years to come. There was no more void in his soul. That sinking feeling, which led one to believe all could be lost as easily as it had been gained, no longer occurred to him. There was something else out there in the dark which puzzled him, something in the very black stuff, which brought him to the realization that for every evil, every bad thought, the seed for something marvelous grew in its place. Out there in the deep of space was not a cold unlit place, but rather an unseen portion of humanity was still unlived, a history unwritten.

It was the very stuff of life, the nectar or juice which encouraged Max to push ahead and face the darkness. It was an unlimited source to be respected. One had so many opportunities to exploit, and then one died either full of regret for not capitalizing on such occasions or content from living a complete rich life.

Max wanted to crack the night open just like a walnut. He wanted the black stuff out there, which went into making the empty space, to reveal its mysterious contents. He imagined splitting open its matter so it would ooze out its properties. He wondered what it was or what it looked like.

Perhaps it was an evil thing, not to be tampered with. Maybe it was composed of the very stuff which kept humans togcthcr, something called love, and that was a good thing, the very glue of life in abundant supply and kept in storage, to be used only when absolutely necessary. When couples were desperately keeping their relationships together and reaching for a way to stay in love, if they really wanted to stay together, they would absorb some of the black stuff into their hearts and share it; pure love shot through the veins, like heroine.

The idea was not so new. It would sustain Max and Marie through the trials of daily life, through the conflict and poison which ran through any concupiscent affair. It had to for there is a hopeful flower which grows under the deep snow of winter, and every spring it promises to deliver its fragrant perfume to those who pay homage to its beauty.

Everyone should be entitled to such happiness. Everyone should be as happy as Max felt that moment, when he thought how magical was the night, asleep under a canopy of stars. He was reminded by something an old friend once had told him.

"Max you have never been able to seize the moment. When certain amorous conditions present themselves, you begin to drift rather than take hold of them. What is keeping you from taking charge, from being the master of your destiny?"

Max knew these were just words. Nevertheless, they filled his ears and mind with a deadening ring of truth. All his life had been spent defending the cause of those weaker than he. It was time to make a stand for what he truly felt inside. He was alone except for Marie; so the only one responsible for his feelings was he.

At first it was a frightening concept to know one had nobody to blame but oneself for the actions one did. Old friends and family were absent in his life, but were they? They continued to haunt him through memory.

No, he thought, that is too easy. Blaming others for one's decisions is using a scapegoat. We must be accountable for our own sins. That is what suffering is for. You endure it, or you succumb to its morose and depressive ability to drag you under until you become too paralyzed with fear to act and feel again.

While Marie was sleeping, Max went for a solitary walk down the Rue Lafontaine. He stopped to gaze up at a clear sky. The constellations were taking their midnight stroll through the heavens, each connected to and determining the others.

His sign, Aquarius the Water Bearer, was nestled between Capricorn the Goat and Pisces the Fish. He absorbed the knowledge from the goat and poured it into the fish, or was it the other way around? Astrologically, the sign of the goat and fish translated to two women who played major roles in his life. If Marie was the fish, who was the goat? Looking for the goat became a source of intrigue for Max. His life was now spent searching for this symbol.

Finding the goat meant completing the missing part of his soul. Perhaps this would finally give him the rest and tranquillity he had long sought. It would put to bed the demons which tried to wrest from him the goodness which was in him. It would give him the chance to expiate the guilt and sin and evil onto the sacrificial goat. What form did this goat have? Was it a woman, a demon, or a religious person like a Christ figure? Whatever it was it would be a cypher or conduit through which Max could escape from the torment and agony of an imperfect world, a world of revenge, deceit, and duplicity. Max was tired of feeling like two people.

Everything seemed to have two signs. Finished with one thing, Max went on to the next. Thinking of one woman led him to the next one. He was never satisfied with the idea of just one woman, one espresso, one good suit of clothes. He always thought of the next one. His actions were indicative of a compulsive behavior disorder. Yet Max always had thought of himself as quite normal.

Was everything a matter of conquering and possessing in order to fully appreciate the object of desire? Perhaps his sights were set too low.

Knowing how fragile the world of material things was, Max became a victim of desire. He fell to the temptations of the flesh as well as having a predilection for the finer, culinary delights. Although he knew this would never bring him any closer to a spiritual awakening, Max realized such a human weakness would catapult him into orbit. Out there in the black space he could be free of choices and an ambivalence which kept haunting him while awake or asleep. Somehow the goat would lead him to it.

Maybe there was nothing wrong with feeling ambivalent. Holding two mutually exclusive beliefs was possible, wasn't it, without losing your mind. There was a God, or there was not a God. Something either is or it isn't. He was in love with Marie, or he wasn't. He could have all the fantasies in the world about a woman or thing, but that would not necessarily bring the situation any closer to reality. What would it take to bring his way of looking at things closer to the way they really were? How could his paintings of scenes in Paris finally come true? Could the figures come to life the way he really saw them? If he could close the gap between his fantasy life and reality, would he be closer to ending the mystery of Max Basset? Should it ever come to an end? Was it not the very thing which sustained him?

For too long the idea of solving the duality which was part of his nature had become a cruel joke. If he got to know someone close enough that he would brush up against their very core, he sometimes would spoil it through distance or a gratuitous sense of humor. It was time to take matters more seriously. He would begin with his relationship with Marie.

The sunlight filtered through the venetian blinds, flooding the apartment with the warmth of a long-lost friend. Max and Marie slept late until Max, as usual, got up to make some breakfast. As he went about his business, frying up some eggs and red peppers, he thought of a time in his childhood.

"Things were not as complicated; feelings were not hard lived by. You acted by instinct, need, desire at the right moment. The moment was king. Now everything is careful deliberation, action and reflection, reassessment, guilt, and occasionally, if you're lucky, you can feel good again." Max grew despondent.

Living took place between the lines of a script. We're all sly actors on the stage of life, but authentic life is realized in the interludes, those magical moments in which we pause to really look around, to see who we are and where we are going, if not to end up exactly in that place from which we started. In our quest for meaning and certainty, we cry out in defiance of death. We compare ourselves to more enduring entities like two-hundred-year-old trees and the Grand Canyon, things which laugh at us on their way to eternity.

In the farthest stretch of the imagination, we come to the boundary zone of human limitation and realize how hungry we are for more. Yet the deeper we know and search out truth, the wiser and more content we grow, the sadder, too.

Max was good at picking up the pieces of the fragmented lives of people, shuffling them like cards, and dealing them out again in new combinations. With hope and with luck they would feel like winners again, full of purpose and pointed toward a meaningful gesture which would change them forever. However, these were figures frozen in pictures, locked in space and time, and constricted by an artist's brushstrokes and fanciful whims.

"Everywhere I want to go, when I get there I realize how it can never be the way I imagined it to be. There is a longing in me to be everywhere at once and yet to remain exactly here. I have fantasies about people, places, and things and wonder if they will ever live up to my expectation of them," he ruminated over coffee.

Max was realizing the pointlessness of this argument, for people will always be on the outside and do what they will. The only moment of intimacy and contact with the significant other was the moment the other left. Then one realized the importance of the other. It was when one set it free to see if it returned again of its own free will. Such a road was a long and arduous one, full of suffering and misunderstanding. The trick was to minimize exercising the poor options and maximize the better ones. This would help Max learn how to seize the moment.

He wanted all the good things to come back to him. He loathed deceit and mendacity. He longed to feel as if he could react instinctively and meet the demands reaching out to him. He was tired of living on the outside.

Marie was instrumental in helping Max find the little boy who was still inside him, crying to be heard again. She showed him the meaning of caring for someone because one chose to from the soul. Yet it took a very special person to realize the simple innocence of unconditional love, one who was young at heart. Although Marie lived on the other side of midnight, she retained that youthful innocence or beautiful naiveté which carried her to the realm of the angels. These privileged few continued to believe love was the answer, not the question. They were sent to earth to show us what we have forgotten in all the confusion: We are here to do God's work, to care for those who are weaker and have lost the way.

What was the way for Max? He was stuck indoors for the day, while outside people, cars, and animals, and time seemed to move in slow motion. Everything was covered in a blanket of virgin snow. It looked white, powdery, and children scooped it up and ate it like ice cream. They were feeding their young bodies with the white stuff which fell from the sky. It was badly needed by the older, dried-up citizens of Paris. They desperately sought a tonic which would metamorphose their bent gait into a purposeful stance, one grounded and not likely to drift into space.

The snow was blown in every direction. It piled up against doorways and cars and prevented access to major transit routes. The city was crawling to a dead stop, but everyone knew inclement weather, no matter how severe, could never kill the spirit of its citizens.

Just as life seemed to have been canceled or written off the history books, Max realized it was just another day. Being thankful and hopeful of the future inspired him to begin painting again. This time he saw men struggling against the futility and boredom of routine labor with slower and more measured steps. The street was filled with vendors opening up their grocery and clothing stores, with a graduated purpose which seemed timeless. It was as if they were defying all known laws of nature.

Rest from the drudgery of habit was noticed in eyes which begged for respite. Other priorities grew in place of personal needs. There were others involved: children and elders too frail to fend for themselves, the sick and destitute, the faint-hearted and insane. Max painted such a collage of characters and captured their hearts on canvas. If we were to witness them coming to life, then we would see how infinitely sad the human plight was.

Max had a dream. Later in the evening he walked along his favorite street, strewn with gas lanterns and full of fashion-conscious pedestrians. He thought of the proprietors of the stores who were to open their businesses first thing in the morning. Despite the bone-cold chill of the night, the many seductive neon lights, and the magic of dusk which promised much more than it could deliver, Max was being led to something beyond his control.

There was an electrical charge which filled an otherwise vacuous existence. It had the promise of reaching that small empty part of the soul which needed living. The night went on its own merciless mission until it tore into his flesh, leaving an open sore for all the sharks to smell. Evil lurked around every corner, waiting to prey on the sick and weak. The past, filled with regrets, was too tempting.

Max was no exception. Being tormented too long by too many horrors had left him vulnerable to the hyenas of the night. The city had its deserts of shifting sands which gave one the impression of a calm surface, while underneath there was a competition for life. Just like the sea, the city had its many currents, some hot and some cold, which carried one beyond one's limitations. Something was learned and quickly forgotten, so new knowledge was absorbed to take the place of old antiquated ideas. Max wanted to move around the next corner and the next and the next until each strange person who confronted him only drove him further into the arms of his sweet Marie.

The pulse of the city reverberated in his mind as the many cars and voices faded into the background. His destination became secondary. What was of paramount importance was reaching somewhere he had already been before. The whole point of his ambulatory exercises was to see if he had missed something previously. Perhaps this time he would notice a new face or an old face which could show him the way to higher ground. He needed a fresh perspective, as any hungry artist will tell you. Max searched for a vision, a window with a view which would take his line of sight beyond this world.

It may have been an escape or flight from reality. It may just have been wanderlust. In reverence for God and creation Max bowed his head to the blue sky, while up above a flock of swallows made a playful circle in flight, showing him the eternal recurrence of things. No matter how he deviated from his chosen path in quest of meaning and truth, there was always the reminder of his mortality through the addiction of habit. He felt comfortable with the thought of returning to Marie or his work, for that matter, knowing he was more sure of himself than before. One had a duty to perfect the skills one was born with in praise of his fellow man. Just as the brush was always waiting for the painter with a keen eye, the trowel for the bricklayer, and the book for the scholar and teacher, so was the labor for the laborer. The only moment it became futile and meaningless was the moment one chose to ignore the situation.

Paying attention to duties is not too much. One thing leads to another, and finishing the task at hand is the only guarantee of immortality. The rest—the sun and sea, the pleasures of the body, chasing the challenges of love although an illusion at its weakest point are still worthwhile projects which employ us constantly. Even if we are confused and often flounder in the amorphous sea of emotional uncertainty, we still have our human dignity to keep us afloat. If we fail to be true to ourselves and our convenant with God, we have our brothers to remind us when we fall. It is our duty to preserve the sanctity of life for the vanquished and the victorious.

As Max turned another corner the sky turned a pale orange color, bringing with it the sense of well-being that one was made for some decent purpose.

He stretched his sights around a tall building to catch the sun as it slowly disappeared behind some thunder clouds. A sadness rose from his heart from knowing this sunset was one of many others, reminding man of his immortality while binding him to habits, to his lot in life. Happy was the man who followed the eternal cycles of life: the seasons, the places of beauty, the carnal and spiritual quests. This lifted him out of his melancholy, as the woodsy smoke from a nearby chimney rose with stealth and filled his lungs with an air of permanence.

The search for love and happiness in a world of conflicting goals and desires breeds contempt and chaos. We must stand back occasionally to look around and see who we really are and where we fit in.

The sun had finally sunk below the horizon yet was still generous enough to emit the last few golden rays so the faint and downhearted would not give up hope. The night moved in as usual, the great equalizer. The wretched and miserable, the good and evil, the ugly and beautiful all became equal in the dark. They all cast the same shadow. They all hid in the small corners of midnight until the light came. However, Max was not an accomplice to the night moves or a victim of its ways. He sought the light even if it was just a reflection from the moon. His task was not to interrupt its journey to earth, as other forces might, but to capture it on canvas and eternalize it. The flow of light had to be continuous and uninterrupted so its power and glory were not enfeebled. He was a true artist.

He spent most of the next day with Marie. They walked through a local park, talked, and laughed away the hours in a carefree contempt for the fleeting daylight. Finally they found a suitable patch of grass where they could rest and enjoy their food. After drinking their ruby red wine they fell back to look up at a limpid blue sky. Was there something beyond its transparency? Max imagined a surreal world of Parisians dressed in fancy costumes and putting on the dog. This was their attempt to feign life, a life of idle worship of religious icons and glossy women in magazines. Wanting to be beyond one's capacity drove the hordes of humanity over the precipice of known reality. Now acting in socially appropriate manners, now smirking as if guarding a secret, they grew obsolete in the face of eternity.

High above the treeline, aimlessly floating in the distance were two balloons making their way toward the countryside. Max and Marie watched them for a while as if their very souls and not the balloons were floating toward the heavens. They wished everyone could be like them, devoted to each other yet free to explore uncharted areas of their souls.

As they lay on the velvety grass, with their hearts deliciously panting and the breeze gently caressing Marie's goose-pimpled skin, a wondrous thought occurred to Max.

"What if this is all there is, Marie? I mean, what if there is nothing more to know? Here we are, my heart next to yours under a blue and green canopy. Everything is right with the world, and my soul is at peace because I have found you! I feel complete, and my search is over."

"Maybe for us it has finally ended. There is a wider world beyond us which we do not understand and perhaps never will. Perhaps it is not for us to pursue. We should be thankful we have each other. God has been good enough to bless us."

"You know, Marie, you have a simple beauty and wisdom of the world, which I take for granted. You have an amazing insight into what I really am. I know I could be happy with you."

After a while they went for a stroll by the pond where the ducks and swans swam unperturbed on the glassy pond. The sky and bulbous white clouds were reflected on the water's surface. Max and Marie gazed into it and saw their images as well. Their reflections became bathed in sunlight, and watching these images flickering on the surface left them in a serene mood.

Suddenly a duck began flapping its wings and taking to the air, disturbing the calm and creating a ripple which seemed to send their images across the pond. Their hearts sank as they watched another part of them drift away into the abyss. Happiness came in waves of opportunity. We must accept this truism and feed on its illusion; we need our illusions just as we need the air to breathe.

Dusk soon came and Max and Marie walked toward that magical part of the evening, where the sky meets the horizon in an explosion of colors. For some reason Max wanted to crack open the sky to see what was behind it. Soon he realized he was asking for too much, knowing what was behind the self-evident. The eye could see but not always know what is self-evident. He pointed to one of the first stars of that evening and told Marie how it seemed to be there in the sky, but really it had ceased to exist years ago. He explained how the star's light had taken millions of years to reach the earth even though the star itself had burned up long before its light had continued to travel through space to reach them on earth.

"In order to really believe it is there, we need to have a sort of blind faith that it will continue to shine even though it is already dead. It is a bond of love which keeps everything right, everything in order and in its place. Without this stability in life we are lost."

Our loyalty to a cause much bigger than life itself, to a belief that all good things will prevail because we have learned to depend on a certain order of things, a certain optimism that all will turn out for the better, must be foremost in our minds. Max and Marie were happy in a God who was wise enough to place stars so far away that even when they died their light would continue to journey toward the earth, bringing joy to humans, beyond their lifetimes.

It was reassuring to know that people like Max and Marie depended on their own individual stars to bring them comfort and peace of mind in times of uncertainty. How could anyone doubt his own existence? How could anyone proclaim life was meaningless, when glaring right at them was living proof that certain things continued to exist even though they were physically dead? Their star was, beyond a doubt, evidence that life itself transcended death; life was stronger then death. First, though, one had to believe in love, which held the whole thing together with a magical glue. Max felt himself drawn toward Marie, under a canopy of sleepy bedroom eyes. They would be up all night rolling like children under the covers.

There is a place in our hearts, a secret place where we live and breathe but into which we don't let many others. We put on our masks and venture into the day, unknowing of the outcome, unaware of the pseudolife we lead, paranoid of our true feelings as if we have something to lose; something is always racing ahead of us.

In the rare moment we catch up to it, we are somewhat surprised to see what it was we were chasing. We were just running after our own selves. Max and Marie had stopped running. They didn't need to hide from each other that small corner of their hearts. They didn't have to pretend or impress anyone. They lived in each other's souls. They breathed the same air and shared the same vision. Life was not running away from them; it needed them as a model of love.

People would stop to watch them in the park or on the street. They stopped to learn what it was like or could be. In the grand race to be somewhere or be something, we have forgotten how to pause, to listen, to see. Once we have gotten over our petty neuroses and achieved a general misery and unhappiness, at least we are in touch with a substantial part of life. We could say we have hit the chord of suffering and confusion we have tried to avoid for too long. Yet we have come too far for too long a journey to end in disappointment. That look of restraint we see in the eyes of others as we walk down the street is the look of tolerance and acceptance. I suppose we have finally learned to wait and see in a patiently enduring way the kind of suffering which will be delivered onto us. This is the courageous stance of the existential hero who accepts his fate only after he has fought to earn the freedom which comes after he has accomplished his duties. This is the plight of the everyday person. He needs to know that despite his many hardships and ordeals, the pain and misunderstanding he experiences at the hands of his fellow man, he still must be reassured that something will be his reward.

For what that something was, Max had spent all his life searching. He knew it lay at the gates of a woman's soul. He needed to enter into that small place where Marie lived and breathed. Every woman had such a secret place and waited for the man with the magic key.

The phone rang at least four times before Max finally volunteered to move across the living room to pick it up. He lifted the receiver toward his ear, greeted the person, but there was no response. Lately this had become a frequent habit of some lonely perverted person whose intention it was to shock Max. At least they were interested in what Max was up to.

Max would pick up the phone and wait, repeat his salutation of "Hello! Hello!" but to no avail. He recalled how this had happened many times before when he was living alone, and a distraught girlfriend with whom he had broken up needed to know and watch his every move—at least until her jealousy and curiosity had worn off.

It was human nature to wonder what the people we are in or out of love with are doing. This last episode had gone much deeper. Max knew that the person making the crank calls needed someone with Max's depth and sensitivity to understand the kind of feelings she was going through.

Naturally he guessed it was a woman, perhaps a beautiful woman whose intricate and delicate disposition was being neglected. Wasn't that always the case with marvelous machines which were not properly oiled? They needed to be constantly primed and ready to run under optimum conditions, or they failed to perform. Just like people who were egomaniacs needed stroking, women especially needed to know they were loved and cared for, or they walked. Men like Max were particularly susceptible to such women.

He only felt vital when he knew he was bringing out the inner beauty of a woman who was floundering. Max was an expert in floundering. He knew all about the depths of misery and sadness. However, he also had learned about the other side, the lighthearted companion of tragedy, the brother of all the sad things in life. He had determined that a real woman kept him from thinking about death, his own death, for that matter. At the same time, she received his charm and manipulations of reality. Every woman wanted a distortion of the truth as if everyday scenes were stretched to the breaking point, played out over and over again until they were worn down and ready for a religious burial. They wanted, or rather begged for, compliments without the deceit and lies. That is, a woman wanted the truth cut up into smaller fragments until she was comfortable with the dishonesty. No matter how well you diagnosed her condition, being the physician of her soul, she didn't want to hear it. The truth is, after all, very boring. One needed to mask it with a good story. Without risking self-delusion, one needed to pretend life was not as horrific as they said it was. It was worse than that. It could be meaningless, with death as the definite proof.

Instead of delivering a rude message to his caller, Max hesitated and just listened for a while. The silent caller on the telephone seemed to be listening, too. They were both listening to the silence. Each of them listened to the abyss between a human relationship. Who would we be if we did not listen to each other's emptiness? How else would we be able to find the love needed to fill the soul which is condemned to roam an empty world?

After a while the silence became deadening. Neither Max nor his mystery caller would divulge their anonymity. Both were afraid of revealing their naked souls to the truth. And what was the truth? It lay there, suspended in the air, on a telephone wire, between here and there. Wherever "there" was could have been on the other side of the world as far as Max was concerned.

Many emotions crossed his mind. He was very angry then sad and full of pity. Gradually he moved onto a deeper level until he realized what a hoax the whole thing was. Life was all so amusing and full of paradox. One moment he was complacently content in his own little love nest with Marie. Now he was curious about the mystery caller. What did she look like; how did she dress, what kind of personality did she have?

He fantasized about having sex with her. She was blonde; then she had black hair. First she was thin and then meaty with a full round bosom and bum. She wore spectacles and her hair was in a bun behind her head. She had long smooth legs with fish-net stockings. Then she changed. She was an oriental woman, petite with a shy and pleasurable smile.

What difference did it make? They were all part of Mother Earth! One simply gave in and fell to earth, into the warm bosom of a saintly woman. The sky opened and spewed out its contents onto earth. Milk and honey flowed through the land, and one absorbed the nectar through the umbilical cord permanently attached to Woman.

Max pictured his ideal woman sitting on a beach on some exotic tropical island. She was facing the surf while the offshore breeze blew through her hair, making it parallel with the turf. The color of her skin and hair were neutral, that is, her hair was neither blonde nor brunette, black, red, nor grey. Her skin tone wasn't fair or dark but simply a healthy tan, hiding any natural blemishes. Why couldn't that woman be Marie?

Why did Max always have to paint over the given state of things? Why did he always have to add the artificial dimension of the artist's brushstrokes to what was seen with the naked eye? This was an obsession of his. He felt he had to extol what was the status quo. He had to add layers of skin, hair, and bone to a banal existence. Did he need a reason to rise above, motivation to reach some higher ground or just return to the place he started?

Max was getting used to insignificance. Marie would provide him with the support he needed during his waking state. He was learning how easy it was to be alive, but the hard part was learning how to die. His nightmares transported him to an underworld for which he was not ready.

In his dreams he drifted into the harsh world of the criminally insane. He was convicted of no crime other than being the individual he was; the painter, the man who dared breach conformity. There among the riffraff, the perverted and deviant subculture flourished a simple survival only because nature had been abolished. It was his subconscious telling him about some unfinished business. It seemed the only recourse to upholding justice was one which led to violent rebellion. This he found in his art.

What made today any different from yesterday? Why should it be any different? The man who lived hoping in some supreme justice to right all the wrongs died an unhappy and disillusioned man. Max stopped hoping in the silver lining of each cloud. He saw his existence as permanently overcast. If the sun came shining through the clouds, it was only out of curiosity, to learn something about his world.

His paintings, born from his faith in humanity in its sheer determination to surmount a scornful god who saw fit to punish man in his dismal state, gave him cause to pursue that which was invisible to the eye. Despite other forces not of this world, which sought to distract him, Max struggled, against the insanity of his nightmares, to erect a new philosophy. It helped bridge the gap between the poverty of hope and the wealth of free will.

With each corner he rounded, with each new horizon at dusk, every street which carried him brought Max back to where he started, where he wanted to be—there in the lap of the world, the womb of indifference. For the rest of his days we know our man to be happy, looking for sweet Marie.

It was a never-ending story. Max arose from a deep sleep, still wondering about the meaning of his dream. He lay there, somewhat disturbed about the nightmare he'd had last night. Convicted of killing his enemies, he had been sent to a hard-core prison. He had engaged in all the usual vices; homosexuality and sodomy, drug addiction, lying and cheating to survive the harsh conditions. He had met interesting characters who looked like movie stars he knew while in his waking state. They all had well-defined personalities, but they lacked one important trait. They were deficient of human compassion.

Max had felt empty as well. He knew they were hollow people and wondered when the nightmare would end. Suddenly he had begun to recognize the people in his dream. They were the ones he met in the barber shop and café. They were the everyday people who inspired him to paint about them. Yet here in the netherworld his painted people were alive. They were no longer confined to his wood-mounted canvas. They breathed the same air as he and roamed his world.

Once they saw their creator, they had run to surround Max and praise him for their lives. He had insisted he was just an artist and the people he painted just artificial representations or symbols of what he saw to be the truth.

In reality he thought people were just the way he painted them, plastic people, fighting to break through to the other side so they could find themselves and function like real people. Real people were not afraid to show their feelings. Underneath their formidable facades, adults like Max and Marie were just scared children running away.

Just like his ancestor Adam, Max was guilty of committing a sin. He was guilty of eating the fruit of life. What was so bad in that? He had eaten all the fruit with impunity, at least until now. He knew the secret of knowledge lay in discovering it at one's own expense. He was not afraid to hold God in contempt if humanity was not served. His classroom was the street, and he became a student-judge full of penance.

Dark clouds were amassing over the City of Lights. Except for a few hopeful signs that the sun was on the other side, the stark contrast between nature and the Parisian skyline left Max in a melancholic mood. Never before had he had such an absurd sense of life. While pondering his delicious lust for life and its pleasures, he also felt a sense of void. Why hide his grasp of the meaninglessness of living day to day? He presented Marie with a challenge. If she loved him, truly loved him, she would give up her temptation to prostitute herself. This was the only thing left for Max to do to fight off lack of meaning in his life. If she agreed to it, he would become grounded in her love.

However, there was something deeper he needed to resolve. Something had plagued his soul since he was a child. He knew it to be vital if he would ever achieve happiness. He also knew the nature of evil lurked in him, as it did in every man. He would be vindicated if he could stab the evil beast in the heart of where it lived, the soul.

Marie had given him the wisdom and patience to conquer the demons within by focusing on his work. Nevertheless this only kept him from his real intention. In order to achieve peace of mind, he had to stare death in the face, his own death, and solve the supreme riddle of life.

Beneath the bone and flesh of every human being is a spirit yearning to be free to express itself. Though every day begins the same way—sunrise, sunset, sunrise, sunset—the opportunity to make a difference is there. Sometimes he didn't know what he would do from one moment to the next. Was there a God in whom he could trust despite all the suffering and hardship, or was he just part of a dream in the mind of a laughing hyena? These were questions which drifted by him from time to time.

He felt his self-confidence beginning to wane. Perhaps it was time for him to leave Paris and take a vacation with Marie. He didn't know. He wasn't sure of anything anymore. At least the demons had left him alone. It was a good time to make his peace with his Creator.

He looked outside his window and saw the bare trees of spring, ready to sprout their buds for another season. Max hoped nature would teach him what he needed to know. It was April in Paris, and the air was filled with a delightful mixture of perfume and the natural scent of flowers. Lovers were walking arm in arm in the parks, in a carefree and timeless gesture of denial.

"Yes, denial!" Max thought out loud.

It was a denial of death and nightmares and demons. Seeing the people walking, talking, and sharing was affirming life, as he suddenly cried, "I am!"

It was enough to know the birds singing and the people's laughter in the parks was a mockery of life's cruel lessons. Max was invigorated with the notion that his fate and the fate of all men rested in the hands of a kind and infinitely suffering God. Sitting alone on the edge of his sofa, he could feel and hear the painful cries of the world screaming for recognition. Yet it was a hopeful cry of humanity which inspired Max. At least it was a sign that there was life instead of death and the abyss.

On the ground outside his apartment was the constant clamoring of life: the street vendors, the peddlers, and the homeless, the lazy, the rich, and the lustful. Inside, in the safety of his room, his soul had a chance to speak to him. Although he went through periods of turbulence, torment, and finally quiescence, he had the courage to survive with dignity. Despite having the bad and ugly side of humanity spit in his face, he had found a way to metamorphose tragedy and hate into artforms. He had dug up the demons from the sinister unconscious depths of his soul to teach him how love could defeat sin.

It took a special courage to dredge up the ghosts of his past, the skeletons in his closet which hung around as if despising that which was still alive in him. He wished a good wind would blow away the cobwebs in his mind which would catch a fleeting memory only to distort the truth about his past. He was guilty, as all of us are from time to time, of turning a vapid experience into something beyond its natural boundaries. Perhaps that was the reason he was such a good surrealistic painter. He turned the torpidity of the walking dead into a celebration of life. He gave his friends from the barber shop and café wings on their feet. His paintings brought meaning to an otherwise vacuous existence.

Yet in his solitary moments of reflection, Max could not escape certain fundamental truths of existence. He knew his work was just a distraction from the inevitable fact that the present, like the past and to a lesser degree the future, was a specter which was doomed to fail where life succeeded.

Where life provided hope and happiness around the corner, the time-abyss proved just as worthy at defeating his initiatives. Though stung by tragedy and sadness all his life, resurrecting hope in the face of the grand equalizer—death or the cessation of the spirit—seemed pretentious and dishonest. Although he was convinced happiness was ephemeral, with long intervals of suffering and something worse than suffering, monotony, his growing uneasiness with bouts of meaninglessness, also brought him closer to the absurd realization that true happiness was just as possible.

All was not lost but, in fact, suspended until he could learn how to make the present remain the present forever. Most of us dwell on the past by distorting and conveniently arranging scenarios to suit our needs. The future is a vast reservoir waiting to be filled by the realization of hopeful dreams. Max was interested in holding the present hostage, that is, making it accountable for the sins and guilt perpetrated against him by his enemies. They would all be tried in the absurd court of the unfolding present.

However, his enemies were just glorified versions of himself. The real enemy was within. While his instincts led him down a certain path, his heart and mind waged a secret war to conquer the vast hinterland of the soul. Outside the city Max was impressed with the lessons of nature. His solitary spot in the cosmos, although strange and forlorn, was subject to the same laws as every single thing, animated or not. Every mineral flake of the mountains, every molecule of water, just like the cells which organized themselves into the making of his hands, were all victims of chance and the temporal flux.

Every reason for being led Max to believe all products of nature had to struggle and compete for their place in the sun. Despite the many ordeals a man must face in his life, the grey hairs on his head and the wrinkles of his skin revealed a unique story of bravery and madness.

What Max was really concerned with was the struggle to understand the nature of evil. The quest would begin within, so he could feel at home with his fellow man, both friend and foe. However, men needed work in order to be perfect. Human beings were paragons of virtues, violent, stupid, and unpredictable at the best of times. What he needed was a better example to draw from. He did not have to look too far because all the ingredients needed to make the supremely dependable person were found in his instincts.

It was his reaction to environmental stimuli which kept him in tune with the outer world. He would walk by the window displays of the stores, and the smartly dressed mannequins seemed to reach out to him for recognition. Above him the neon signs winked and blinked in measure with his step. All the symbols directed Max toward the end of the street. Max reached the end of the curb and gazed toward the horizon during his favorite time of the day. He wondered where the street ended and the horizon began? He concluded that it was an optical illusion. He entertained the absurd notion that there were other misleading images presented to his vision—all the more reason he should paint what he felt was the truth about his perception of reality.

Walking down the concrete street in his sandals liberated him from his daily routine. If a camera had been pointed at him, the lens would have shown a man walking in slow motion with a careful yet deliberate step. Each stride covered some territory within a certain time frame.

However, it was something else that set Max apart from most men. It was his ability to fit in anywhere. He could mingle with any social group, with a smoothness and ease which stated that he belonged.

He stopped and sat with his friends at the café or barber shop for hours, meticulously digesting morsels of conversation. After listening for a while, he had the impression that what was at stake was the search for the cure for evil.

Everyone had an opinion, and everyone had prepared a new reason to complain that they were being cheated by life's unfairness. He found it curious how most of these people passively accepted this truth. Rather than confront the enemy or the evil whose sole aim was to conquer the uncharted territory of the soul, most people waited for it to pass them by and hoped they would never share the brunt of evil forces. Max, on the other hand, would walk but never run away from the nature of malice. He simply stayed a few steps ahead of its onslaught. Today was simply another day. Tomorrow was another world already preparing its own horrors as well as its heights to climb.

On his walks he reflected on the nature and origin of evil and concluded that it was derived from having too much time on one's hands. It was born during monotonous periods, when people had time to fabricate and pass on malicious schemes and lies to others willing to participate. Just as long, protracted, and usually unnecessary wars were begun by governments, people were of the same body and mind.

Concomitantly, we have the development of the infinite circle of myth and reason. We fall prey to either myth, which travels through time in the shape of the human story, or reason, which has its own timetable. We believe in myths or stories which agree with our nature. Importantly, we give credence to reason if we dare search for the truth, the latter way being the more difficult one and the road often less traveled.

Which road was Max taking? If he listened to his heart, he would immerse himself in the smoke-filled cafés and bars of Paris, gathering enough tragic stories to break the heart of Jesus. However, his mind and soul belonged to the endless street which led him out of the city and toward the horizon. His obsession with that unspeakable wish to overcome his own intellectual limitations won him the honor of flirting with the gods. They created distance, while man continued to weave his mythological reasons for being.

On the advice of many friends, Max would prepare for certain events in the future. Yet, as the day of celebration would near, he would realize how absurd it was to live in anticipation of some future event. Most people lived this way in the hope that all wrongs perpetrated against them in the past would be eliminated forever by their newfound happiness. The future held no such promises. It is we who filled this future void with dreams and fantasies in order to give meaning to the unlived portions of our vacuous lives. The past remains unclear yet beckons us out of our unconscious sleep to study what is the best way to live a perfect day or afternoon or evening. That way we bury the notion of tomorrow or infinity once and for all and act as if we are gods, immune to judgment because we have transcended the space and time required to commit heinous crimes of the heart. These include hypocrisy, cheating, and lying, and worst of all, bearing false witness to a friend.

This was the way Max walked down his beloved boulevards of Paris, a free man immune to judgment because he alone was responsible for every choice; and he alone would suffer or rise to dizzying heights, depending on the outcome of that choice. Yet he was profoundly affected by the absurdity of any lasting joy. His partner Marie rekindled his soul; that only a woman could do. Nevertheless, that sense of completeness was fleeting, and soon Max would be in his own world again, devoid of any permanent meaning in life.

In that sense he could never be a totally free person because he was unable to surmount that otherness in being or those forces outside himself which waged a relentless war to conquer his soul. Soon death would seal his fate, and like an idiot going to his grave, he would still not know the real reason for his existence. Few of us admit such things to ourselves. We go about our business to distract our full attention away from the crucial questions confronting us day to day. Max felt this was a dishonest way to live. Perhaps the only meaning to be found is that which comes to us just before we contemplate suicide. That reason, like a pendulum swinging on a thin string, is the only thing keeping us alive. We spend our lives searching for such meaningful reasons to live, but when we cannot find a good reason to sustain us, that sends us into a deep despair.

His work gave him meaning. Marie gave him the meaning to pursue the paradoxical truths of life. He feared for the lack of power he had to alter certain courses. He would not feel guilty for those things he could not change. World events were outside his domain. They would evolve with or without his influence. Max geared his efforts toward the expiation of his own guilt and sins, for being in the human mix guaranteed that he would sooner or later offend or be offended by others seeking to dominate and replace him. This he found to be a curious habit of human beings. It was part of the human story to impose values and beliefs on others as if we had an inside scoop on how to live. Perhaps we were all inferior gods, wanting to be humans. Max definitely knew he could never be like God, so it was better to wear the human face God would have if He were human.

The faces Max saw as he walked down the street were expressions frozen against a timeless background. He could have been in any part of the world, and after a while the same human setting would be sure to unfold. People wanted to belong somewhere, people with faces and names. The tragedy is that we identify much more easily without problems than with our human advantage at solving them.

Max knew he was no different from anyone else trying to escape the insanity of the human paradox. How could so many people living and sharing the same space of the city be so utterly cut off from each other? Yes, there was some attempt at communication, especially in a culture which shared the same food, customs, and values. Yet beyond the cultural norms there was a lack of human understanding. It was this overwhelming feeling of isolation Max felt when he stared at the horizon beyond the street. The street would run out of concrete, and then the void would set in, he alone against the surreal skyline of Paris. A thousand eyes lit up office buildings and passively watched a man walking and living in a city whose roads led back toward its center, not permitting any escape.

Max was searching for the escape route away from the madness of human alienation. He concluded that nobody could serve two causes simultaneously, at least not successfully. Perhaps this was the downfall of people who tried to be good for everyone. It was impossible to serve two gods at once, be an expediter of good and evil, be happy and sad. One was either one or the other. The gray area was left for madmen to live in. One could not go through life being a disciple of God and Satan. Max was too exhausted to act on such serious decisions. He chose to react rather than act on impulse. Learning how to wait was one of the hardest disciplines in the world. Now hesitant, then striking out boldly where no one had dared before, was man's glory or folly, depending on how kindly or cruelly fate would write the story.

There was Max, a curious walking contradiction, aimless and forlorn like most of his contemporaries, searching for a reason to live beyond the end of the street. An authentic existence surely was around the next corner. At dusk his shadow began to loom against the wall of a bank as he rounded a corner. He stared at it for a while and noticed how much larger it was than he. This was the way he wanted to see himself. He wanted to tower above everyone else. He wanted to be a moral giant in a land of slimy hypocrites and mental midgets. This was the sort of exercise in self-delusion in which alienated people of the modern age participated.

Searching for an equal playing field in which all the players were fair and abided by the rules of honor could be asking for too much. Max knew justice was administered by those who had the power to inflict their own rules on the weak and the oppressed. Was this why he was alone to wander in a lost paradise of failed humanity? The human experiment to find and live in a perfect world had failed the moment we went against the rules set by our Creator long ago. The rest of time had been spent in wanderlust and solipsism, each man equally misunderstood by his fellow man, each of us drowning in a sea of moral iniquity. This failed human drama will never play to its bittersweet end until a scornful god decides to intervene in human affairs. Until then we are left to our own devices, scrambling toward elusive goals and justice for all. These impossible demands we ask from each other in a world which God has abandoned.

He has given us souls. We are free to write our destiny although it has already been written. Max was confident every person struggled to achieve some sort of freedom from oppression. Governments and people oppressed each other. We oppress ourselves most of all. We should never abandon character and virtue. This is something to fight for. Max felt the pressure of change in a transitory world of fleeting images. This was what he captured on canvas despite the urge to remain the same. Man extolled reality, and this was what Max painted. It was men locked by their past and rooted in the present. While former selves dissolved into the vapor trails of the past, new versions of the self grew in their places. A metamorphosis in character erupted from the mist of time, and like the phoenix rising out of the ashes of death, man was constantly redefining himself, being reborn again and again.

The people and places Max painted were not desperate people subjected to mischance and folly. They were fragmented vectors pointing toward the hopeful illusion of the future. Their images, eroded by time and failure, were frozen against the shifting background of the streets. In this case the street was victorious. Just as the mountains try to defeat man's spirit, those things which outlast us make our lives seem meaningless. It was the streets, mountains, and all those things which seem permanently pitted against the will that Max was interested in surmounting.

Once again he walked down the street, but this time he held Marie's hand. It was dusk, and the air held up the damp sweetness of spring. They walked to the edge of the street and gazed at a setting sun nestled between two large buildings. For a moment Max felt his heart soaring toward the falling sky. Just before he took flight, Marie clutched his arm and brought him down to earth. She gently nudged his erect member, reaffirming his dubious existence. This was all the proof he needed that life was worth living.

There they stood arm in arm, heart to heart while a red sun dropped from an orange and blue sky. They made a secret connection with this eternal configuration as if they lived it over and over again, life after life.

From time to time Max thought of previously "failed" love affairs. He recollected the way they ended. Yet he knew in his heart of hearts that nothing was over until it was over. We all left situations unresolved, and Max was no exception. He had bittersweet memories, but most of them were good. The relationships were not whole because both he and his partners were unsettled with themselves. Something always had come between them, and sooner or later they had drifted usually apart from each other. He thought how convenient it was to be able to selectively remember the good over the bad. He was a survivor, and survivors knew how to keep the good and throw out the bad. The instinct of self-preservation demanded it, and that which we lack which is good for us, we seek until we find. Max found it in Marie, and she became a secret holder of the goodness Max had long searched for all his life.

There we have it! Man coming to the end of his long search for meaning and happiness is no small matter. Yet is it the end or the beginning of some new purpose? We never work in secret, away from the maddening throngs of humanity. We must be in concert with our Creator. His eyes gaze down from the heavens in curious indifference perhaps and out of scorn for our pitiable lives. Nevertheless, there must be some small mysterious connection there in the dark, between heaven and hell, between the earth and falling sky, which binds man to his mission. Yes, there at the edge of the street, the end of the ocean or the precipice of the mountain, man forges his trust in a power higher than himself.

Max had made this secret pact with this superpower the moment he had stepped into the light of day and the time he had watched it slip away into dusk. There is no other purpose in man but to be alive and survive day to day with dignity and courage. This solidifies his character which yields to the virtue which is made in God's image.

If we be specks in a vast universe, so be it. We make a difference the moment our conscience awakens to the sights, sounds, and images of this not-so-distant world. Max painted what he saw, heard, and felt in his heart if only to resurrect in his fellow man a new hope and spirit to transcend the mediocrity which sometimes widens and deepens the abyss between what man is and what he could be?